ISBN 978-1-7379764-2-4

DEDICATION

This book is dedicated to my children, Leah and Marshall II, and my grandchildren, Trey, Vyolette, Legend and Marshall III

I believe that you are the reason I was placed on this earth, and you are the justification for each breath that I take

I am so proud of each and every one of you

Never allow doubt in yourself or your abilities to keep you from accomplishing your dreams

Because behind every self-made successful person lays a vast wasteland of failures; that person just kept trying until they got it right!

Love,

Mom

Grandmama

CONTENTS

Praise for

I AM A DAHOMEY WARRIOR!

✶✶✶✶✶

"Fierce and Fearless"
Dionne D Hunter is a wise, warm, and fierce firebrand of a poet and performer, so I had high expectations for her I am a Dahomey Warrior, and I was not disappointed. Her prose is lean and muscular and for many reasons her story is the type we need more of. I'm a fan and expect you will be too.
Reviewer: John Burroughs, Ohio Beat Poet

Laureate, and author of Rattle and Numb

✭✭✭✭

"A celebration of a history that needs to be told and re-told."

Don't do as I did when you read Dionne Hunter's narrative poem. "I AM A Dahomey Warrior. I raced through it too quickly because I was so compelled to find out what happened next. Instead, slowly savor the lyrical notes Hunter strikes, as she unfolds the story of a girl whose desire to become a Dahomey warrior is driven by both tragedy and pride.

For some, Hunter's poem will be a lesson for those who do not know of the fierce beauty of the Dahomey warriors, for others it's a celebration of a history that needs to be told and re-told. Hunter takes her place with the griots of the past, as she captures the bravery of the Dahomey warriors, as well as their struggle to be equal to all, in a clear, compelling way.

"I AM A Dahomey Warrior," is spare, eloquent telling of a tale that might just inspire a new generation to not only better understand the past but use it as an inspiration for the future.

Reviewer: Dan Polletta is a veteran broadcaster and writer, who frequently reports on arts and culture in Northeast Ohio.

✦✦✦✦✦

"You can almost hear the protagonist's heart beating…"

You can almost hear the protagonist's heart beating, and occasionally breaking, in this gripping journey from the crushed innocence of childhood to the battle-scarred woman now reflecting back on her life. Dionne D. Hunter writes with such passion and detail, pulling us completely into the story, almost enough to pierce our skin with those devil thorns.

Reviewer: Keith Allison, Poet and Author of What if the Shoe Were on the Other Hoof? and Screaming with My Indoor Voice

" A story to inspire"

A fictional narrative poem that takes place in a true historical setting, I Am a Dahomey Warrior highlights key survival moments of loss and triumph in the life of a strong, resourceful African heroine and the tribe she formidably defends. Much like the main character of the story, author Dionne D. Hunter strives to celebrate, honor, and preserve her African heritage by imparting stories of positive role models to future generations. A story to inspire many to overcome their own challenges and to encourage interest in learning more about African History, this story is a vital treasure to revisit and share often.

Reviewer: Jen Pezzo - Author of Imaginary Conversations (The Poet's Haven) and Lucid Brightenings (Writing Knights Press)

$$\star\star\star\star\star$$

"She is not just telling a story; she is sharing a soul."

Ms. Hunter's voice is powerful, and she wields it with wisdom, sophistication, dignity, and purpose. She is a modern-day history teacher, blending in the past and making it connect with current events. Her writing is sincere and honest and humble, respectfully provocative, and unapologetic. She commands the reader's attention with her attention to detail, she compels you to find the truth in yourself through her story, through her experience and the experience of others. She is not just telling a story; she is sharing a soul. She is keeping the echo of a voice alive, for the preservation of the truth, hope and love.

Reviewer: Jason F Blakely, Sr.- Poet and Publisher - Poetry Is Life Publishing

DEFINITION

This is my take on the Narrative Poetry and Short Story form. I see this piece as a hybrid form of writing in which a narrative with structural and stylistic similarities to traditional Storytelling is told with the aid of Poetry

Chapter One

We are Fon
We lived near Abomey in what was
known as the Kingdom of Dahomey in
West Africa, now called Benin
We have rich traditions and a proud
history
Both of which are passed down from
generation to generation
Magnificently recounted by Griots

Many times, I have heard the chronicling
of days long past

My favorites being stories of the fearless
female Elephant Hunters
Detailed accounts of their bravery and
self-sacrifice are regular topics of any
Griot as villagers young and old listen
intently

In my youth, during the day men tended
crops, and women gathered food

However, both men and women were also
encouraged to take up arms
So many of our men had been lost, women had no choice but to stand their ground, fending for themselves and their families
With that being said, women still were not seen as men's equal and to improve our standard of living, women had to marry well or enlist into the infantry
However, even though we were not thought of as equal to men, it has always been believed that we are more loyal and trustworthy in battle due to our maternal instincts

CHAPTER TWO

Before dawn I was awakened by the
sound of a crackling fire, lowered
voices, and footsteps
I rose excitedly, anticipation brewing
Marveling as I secretly viewed all the
activity surrounding me
A Huntress, conveying orders, albeit, in
a hushed tone, moved from place to
place, gathering equipment
She was tall and slender with defined
muscles well-proportioned to her
curvaceous frame
Her eyes held a kindness that did not
match the creases that etched their way
across her brow
Others, just as stately as she, answered
to her call

They all seemed to have the same
objective in mind, obviously hurrying but
taking care not to disturb the other
villagers as they readied themselves for
the day's adventure

I fought to stay awake
Desperate to witness the group's
departure
As I propped my head up for a better
view, I heard a rustle behind me
Next thing I knew, my little sister was
cozying up to me
"What are you looking at?" she asked
"Go back to sleep!" I muttered
"I can't. I'm not sleepy," she whined

Even in the dark, I could tell that she
cocked her head over to one side as
she looked up at me.
She begged, "Tell me about the great
Elephant Hunter adventure." "The one
the Griot shared the other night."
I shrugged, "Why, so you can have
nightmares and tell on me?"
"Anyway, can't you see I'm busy!"

"I promise, I won't say a word." "Please!"
She begged, her voice squeaking.

Fixing my gaze on one of the women
Using my elbow and arm as support, I
propped my head up
Finally, I gave in, I really could not
resist!
I began reciting just as I had heard the
Griot repeat so many times before

CHAPTER THREE

Concealed by vegetation
Spears in hand
A configuration of female Huntresses lay
in wait
Listening actively
Noticing the forest alive with all its
brilliancy
Water ebbing through a neighboring
stream
While insects traveled flower-to-flower
pollenating only the most colorful of the
bounty
For a moment, the commander was
taken back to more innocent times

She reminisced of times in her youth
when she set quiet scenes, such as
these, to canvass

Shrubbery breaking under heavy weight
Snapped her back to present day
The prey ambled along the riverbank
Bulls leading, calves following behind
A change in strategy was needed
The Warriors shifted their attack to the
rear
Elephants pivoted to meet the threat
Ghastly trumpeting erupted
Spears infiltrated!
Ivory impaled!
Two fearless foes converged!
Elephants concerned only with
protecting their young
Huntresses thinking only of the mothers
relying on them to feed theirs

Then terrible screams
The Commander watched in horror as
three of her sister warriors were gorged
and trampled
Unimaginable horrors

But the Commander had no choice but
to continue, while showing no fear
Even though her tears flowed
uncontrollably, she called out orders,
pushing onward
Finally, the Huntresses separated a calf
from the herd
Triumph!
The Commander wiped blood, sweat
and entrails from her brow

Looking left to right she nodded
approval towards her surviving regiment
And they began the long trek home
The weight of calf carcass and their
fallen soldiers on their backs
As the regiment approached, they heard
chants carried over the wind
- We Will Never Forget Our Sisters- We
Will Never Forget the Cost You Bear –
- We Will Never Forget Our Sisters- We
Will Never Forget the Cost You Bear –

CHAPTER FOUR

Heavy breathing
I looked down at my sister and chuckled
to myself
Wondering how she could fall asleep
during such an exciting story
Glancing back out toward where I had
last seen the Huntresses
I noticed they had moved on
I was so engrossed in my tale, I missed
their departure
And I knew they were off starting their
own adventure
Moments later I too was fast asleep

My mama said, "Shuuushhh!" "Don't
make a sound"
As she gathered my sister and I
together
"Come on! Hurry! Get up!" She
whispered excitedly
Still half asleep, I could now make out
what sounded like cries for help along
with the sound of running feet
I did not understand what was
happening
But we followed closely behind my
mama as directed
Whatever was happening I knew she
would take care of us
She always had
Ever since my father had been killed
Mama was our protector
Having a very slight build, it seemed to
me, a strong wind could carry her away
without much effort
But I knew she loved us with all her
heart, and she would never let anything
happen to us
We moved quickly

But suddenly there was a man standing
in front of her
My mama screamed, shocked by his
appearance
He grabbed her by the arm
They struggled
I didn't know what to do
As I stood embracing my sister
I noticed he wore a brightly colored,
baggy shirt which had a scattered
pattern and weaved neck
His trousers were long but stopped just
above the ankle
I recognized these types of garments
He was from the Yoruba tribe

Pulling my sister away from me
I looked into her big brown eyes and
said, "Stay here, I must help mama!"
I ran to my mother's side, kicking the
man and screaming for him to let her go
But he wouldn't
He slapped me, knocking me to the
ground and began dragging my mother
toward a group of women who were
being bound and led away

My mother managed to take out her
knife
Driving the blade deep into his shoulder
He stopped for a moment
It seemed more out of shock than pain
The next thing I remember is hearing an
awful sound
And seeing my mother go limp in his
arms
He had snapped her neck
My mama was dead
He tossed her aside
Letting her body fall to the ground with a
thud
Like she was little more than garbage

I looked back at my sister, she stood
there in shock
I turned back to my mother
I pushed the thought of her being dead
out of my head, dropping to the ground,
placing her head in my lap
I reasoned that she must be acting in an
attempt to throw the man off track
I began shaking her
Begging her to rise

I screamed, "Mama, please wake up, please open your eyes!"

The man attempted to drag me away from her
But I began kicking wildly and biting so much that he moved to easier prey, my sister!
He picked her up and walked toward the crowd
Sending two other younger-looking men back for me

I saw what was happening!
I saw him grab my sister!
But I couldn't comprehend it, nothing was registering!
I wanted to help my sister!
Her screams were deafening!
But I also wanted my mama to get up
I couldn't think straight
I couldn't leave my mama
As my mind whirled out of control
My Sister's screams moved further and further away

Through my tears I saw the two men
coming near
At that moment I looked down at mama
And she still wouldn't move, her eyes
remained closed, her body limp
"No, no, no, no! I will not leave you
laying here in the dirt!" I screamed!
Still holding her head in my lap
I rocked back and forth
The men were almost upon me
I had a choice to make!
I carefully placed my mama's head
down upon the earth and then I fled
I ran, as my sister's grisly cries echoed
in my ears
I ran

CHAPTER FIVE

As darkness descended
I sat quietly sobbing, rocking myself
back and forth
I had found a hollow tree and claimed it
as my hiding place
I heard footsteps approaching
I was cautious because hours ago I had
come to the horrible realization that I
was the only one who had escaped
capture
I gathered myself
Summoning enough courage to venture
out
Thankfully, I could see the hunting party
moving towards my direction, trophy in
tow

Covered in dirt and dried tears I ran to meet them
Stumbling over rocks and fallen branches as I went

As I approached, I could see that the group was shocked by my appearance
The lead Huntress pulled me close to her
Asking questions, trying to determine why I was in such a state
I relayed the day's events
My eyes brimming with shame

The Huntress pulled me closer, hugging me tightly
She looked down at me with dark piercing eyes and said,
"None of this is your fault."
"Today you are only a child."
"You did what you were able to do, Survive!"
"Tomorrow, we will search for your sister and the other villagers."
"Tonight, we bury your mama."

I looked sternly into the Huntress's eyes, and said with conviction, "I am going to be a warrior like you someday!"

I believed with all my heart that if the Huntress and her Sister Warriors had been in the village the outcome of the attack would have been vastly different

The Huntress put her hand on my shoulder and said,
"You were spared for a reason."
"I believe that you will make the Ancestors, including your mother and father, very proud."
"And when your time finally comes to join our forbearers"
"You will rest easy in the knowledge that you have lived a purposeful life"
"A life worth saving"
"But even more importantly, when the time is right"
"Yours will be a life worth dying for"

.

CHAPTER SIX

I watch the evening sky blossom into
shades of coral
Sun meeting the water's edge
I have observed this scene hundreds of
times before
Still somehow, I expect steam to drift
towards the heavens
As the sun descends just beneath the
horizon into the lagoon
But as usual, it customarily retires,
bereft of fanfare

Resting, arms wrapped loosely around
legs
I try to relax, as the cool waters of the
Porto-Novo wash over me

Remnants from the waning sun set the
tranquil blue waves to a sparkle as joyful
sounds linger carelessly in the air

My Sisters in arms celebrate the
competition to come
I choose to be alone
Mentally preparing
My own thoughts the only conversations
I care to entertain, right now

As my mind wanders
Memories of joyous times spent with my
mother, father, and little sister flood over
me
Those were times before I knew the
meaning or weight of grief
I wonder to myself, if my mama could
see me now, would she recognize me?
I am no longer the awkward 10-year-old
girl I used to be
But then I ask myself the same question
I have asked over and over and over
again
I wonder if my mother would be proud of
me

Although I try to push the thought away
My mind drifts to my final memory of my
sister
I still hear her cries echoing in my mind
Although the Huntresses searched, they
were never able to find her or any of the
other villagers
I have no idea of her fate and I wonder,
if by some miracle she were still alive,
could she, would she, ever forgive me?

CHAPTER SEVEN

I finally succeed in pushing thoughts of
my family out of my mind
But I am only able to do so by thinking
of the history of the land that surrounds
me
This area is known for the opulence of
the land, its resources, and what we
have been told is an exotic allure of our
raven-skinned women
All of which attracts the roving eyes of
marauders both foreign and domestic
Each wishing to overthrow our crown
So, none were surprised when Queen
Hangbe began utilizing Female
Elephant Hunters as her personal guard

Nor were any surprised as they evolved into a feared elite fighting force

The only cause for bewilderment, at least in my eyes
Is that I am on the cusp of joining the ranks of those tenacious women

Gazing off into the firmament
Doubt occurs amongst my thoughts
Yes, I have withstood days, alone, in the wilderness surviving off the land
I've even mastered hand to hand combat
But we have been warned that the challenges that await test more than our competitive spirit and stamina, they examine our mental fortitude
I wonder if I am woman enough to succeed
But I vow to the Ancestors to give my all and leave nothing on the field of competition

CHAPTER Eight

Move! Faster! She must not pass you!
Three miles up, over and under various
obstacles
The African Sun searing down into my
melanin
I don't know how but I increase my
pace, just as the moat comes into view

My heart feels as though it will pound
through my chest wall
Thirty paces to go
Thoughts race, like Lion after Antelope
Twenty-five paces
Breathe!
Twenty paces
Pain is the enemy, and must be
defeated at all cost
Ten paces
The strength of my Ancestors ascends
upon me
Five paces
Pushing off using my back leg, I jump
Clearing the moat
Now, there is nothing between my
ultimate defeat or victory except my own
willpower and a nine-foot acacia
covered wall

Acacia trees, are veiled with razor sharp
thorns
Branches of one such tree shroud the
barricade

Glancing behind me
I see my closest pursuer clear the moat
Leaving no time to consider the devilish
thorns that await, I leap!
Beginning my climb
Pulling myself up onto the branches
My hands and feet instantly begin to
bleed
Brilliant explosions of pain erupt
But I push onward
Picturing my seven-year-old sister atop
the wall
Crying out
Begging me for rescue
I will not fail her this time!

I continue my climb
The taste of sweat and blood
commingling
Every move manifesting a new tear to
once pristine skin
My cleavage now raw, still I carry on
Pushed on by the imagined cries of my
sister

Finally, I reach the highest point
Dragging myself up and over
I drop to awaiting ground
I am no more than tenderized meat
But still, I feel relieved
I have endured unimaginable pain
However, I never murmured a sound
A requirement for successful completion
of the trial
The unit leader, a woman of mahogany
complexion
Stands off to the side observing
Her dignified manner matched only by
her majestic beauty
Suddenly she motions toward me
signaling my success
I stand, absorbing the moment
A bloody mess, I'm astonished by my
accomplishment
Only fifteen of fifty have realized our
dream, this day

As we congregate
The three fastest are called

We approach and are presented
elaborately braided acacia twigs,
fashioned into belts
A great honor, indeed!
As the first to finish, the largest is
awarded to me

Devil thorns on full display
The sash is cinched around my waist
Piercing directly into the toned muscled
flesh of my abdomen
Crimson droplets surge to the surface,
escaping, and begin collecting at my
feet
I barely notice
I feel only pride
I raise my fist towards the sky and shout
for the very first time
"I am a Dahomey Warrior!"

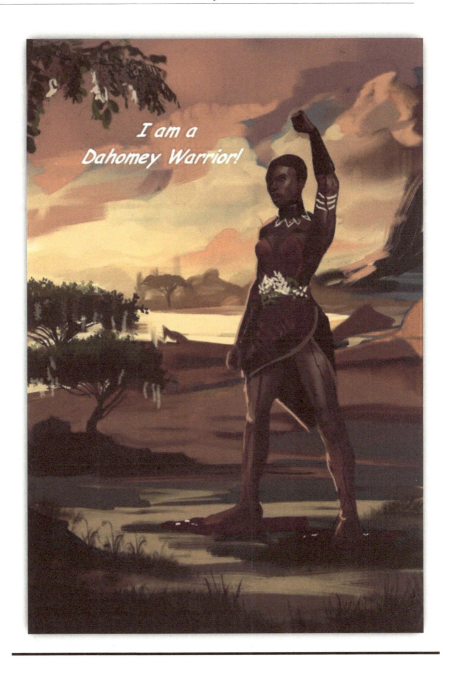

CHAPTER NINE

Decades have passed
I have the scars to prove it
Along with bronzed skin, wrinkled and
leathery
A reward many of my fellow Warriors
never lived long enough to receive
Years ago, I enlisted in the service of
my country, the Kingdom of Dahomey
I honed my combat skills battling
factions of the Yoruba and Egba tribes
And used those opportunities to search
for my sister
I was never able to bring her home, so, I
channeled all the rage and pain from my
childhood into future confrontations
I proved to be a fierce combatant and
leader and ascended ranks quickly

Then I became aware of a new challenge
European Colonists, arriving to our shores with their pale faces, long handled bayonets, and flintlocks

Intense battles ensued
Years passed
Their superior firepower was matched only by the sheer number and ferocity of our male warriors
But as our female militia joined the fray, the added pressure, strategic planning, and our pure savagery began to wear down the foreign marauders
During those grisly battles
The Legend of the female Dahomey Warrior was born

.

CHAPTER TEN

Whispers of the Europeans' interest in a truce were proven to be more than just idle chatter when King Ghezo directed me, his most trusted General to secure the promised peace accord

Our all-female elite fighting force marched 100 miles to meet the Frenchmen
We boasted five Battalions
2500 troops in all
Our most feared regiments in the foreground
Elephant Hunters, close quarter fighters, carrying long spears and short swords

Reapers, wielding two-foot-long razors
able to split men in half with a single
blow

As I negotiated finite details of the truce
with my counterpart
My troops stood ready, as did his
However, this man speaking on, what
he called the unbearable heat of Africa
Reminisced of comforts awaiting him
upon his return to France
He seemed so fragile to me
Not worthy of my efforts
But it was not my place to second guess
my King

I accomplished the goal, the truce was
signed
And we shared a celebratory drink
Then the unthinkable happened
This man looked at me
Not as a soldier
His eyes seemed to undress me as he
reached out grabbing me by the waist
pulling me towards him
I felt disgust rise within me as he spoke

"My dear, you are absolutely captivating, slender yet so shapely"
"With such a proud demeanor; you must be your King's favorite"
"What an exquisite specimen; I think I will call you my African Amazon"
He then attempted to place his hand on my chin
I stepped back and simultaneously grabbed his hand and arm
Reversing his position and pulling him toward me
I placed my knife to his throat, blood trickled down his neck as he gasped in shock
To speak to me; of me
In such a hedonistic manner
I thought of how easy it would be to slit his throat
Splattering blood onto anyone within six feet
They needed to learn respect
Right now! This second!
But today was not my day to teach him manners

Villagers, troops, and my King were
counting on me
And the truce had already been signed
Only by grace of the Ancestors did I
have strength enough to allow him
another breath

.

CHAPTER ELEVEN

Trade between our countries ensued
and there was peace
For awhile
But as time passed the French proved
to be arrogant and untrustworthy
Allowing me to meet the man who
disrespected me once more
This time on the field of battle
Locking eyes
We both realized this would be the last
time we would meet in this life
I charged
He stood his ground
Aiming his rifle in my direction
He took his shot
The bullet grazing my cheek
All at once I was upon him

He attacked
Thrusting his bayonet forward with all
his might
Piercing the skin along the side of my
ribcage

I rotated, swinging my sword
And with one fatal swoop his head was
detached from his shoulders
His body fell to one side
As his head fell to the other
Bouncing just a little before settling into
the dust

Reaching down, I grabbed a hand full of
his hair
I raised his head to eye level
His gaze now blank
I stared into his eyes
and said,
"I am not your Amazon!"
"I am a Dahomey Warrior!"
I held his head high
The last of his still warm blood drizzling
down the left side of my body
Charging forth

Blade in hand
I could see looks of horror flash across
the faces of his men as they realized
their mortality was fast approaching its
end

.

CHAPTER Twelve

All my adult life
I have been a warrior
Fighting for the sovereignty of the
kingdom in which I live
Fighting for my honor
Fighting for my legacy

Though my proudest moments were off
the battlefield
They were the times I noticed the glint in
a young girl's eye
As she caught sight of me and my Sister
Warriors
As we traveled the Kingdom mentoring
and teaching

Becoming a warrior changed my life
Allowing me to nurture my protective
nature
While lifting me out of poverty

As a Female Dahomey Warrior, I, and
all others like me
Had to ceremonially marry the King

That also included taking a vow of
celibacy
Meaning I would have no children of my
own
Therefore, I felt a responsibility to all the
children of the Kingdom

My goal was to exemplify honesty,
loyalty, and integrity
While challenging village hierarchy and
biases toward women

I like to believe it was not only my
strength and cunning on the battlefield
that set me apart but also, my
willingness to be a role model to young
girls
So many times, I explained that they
could do and be whatever they chose
A teacher, healer, warrior, wife, mother,
or leader
Emphasizing that all is within their reach
and that their past does not define them
It merely helps to strengthen them for
what is to come

So here I am, in my 100th year
In a weakened state
Yet not alone
Surrounded by those who love and
respect me
Knowing, I have done all that I could do
to ensure young girls understand the
strength that lies within their voice

So, as I lay here, the last glimmer of
light fading from my eyes
I whisper, to those surrounding me,
"Always remember we are not
Amazons"
"We are greater, authentic, and
unparalleled"
"Never allow them to erase us from
history"
"We are and will forever be Dahomey
Warriors!"

Dahomey Amazons, Amazon Warriors, Female Soldiers or Female Warriors (Benin) 1890s. Aka Mino, they were a Fon all-female military regiment. Vintage Illustration or Engraving 1897

More information:
This image could have imperfections as it's either historical or reportage.
Location: Kingdom of Dahomey, now the Republic of Benin

ABOUT THE AUTHOR

Dionne D Hunter is originally from Birmingham, Alabama, but has also called Ohio and North Carolina home.

After the sudden death of her mother, Ms. Hunter was raised by her widowed father, who strove to raise her to be self-reliant and proud of her African American heritage.

He also encouraged her to read; and read she did, everything including poetry, sci fi, horror and romance. She fell in love with the art of storytelling and would spend hours weaving adventurous tales to entertain her siblings.

As a United States Navy Veteran, mother of two and grandmother of 4, Ms. Hunter has gravitated to

Spoken Word as an expression of her emotions and ideals.

Her work has been included in anthologies published by Writing Knights, The Poet's Haven, and Crisis Chronicles Press. Her Spoken Word videos have been selected to be screened during the 9th International Video Poetry Festival in Athens, Greece, and the 2021 Raleigh Films and Art Festival in North Carolina as well as placing third for Best Spoken Word Performance during the 2021 Monologues and Poetry International Film Festival.

You may learn more about Ms. Hunter by visiting www.dionnehunter.org and you may email her at info@dionnehunter.org

Lightning Source UK Ltd.
Milton Keynes UK
UKHW050819020323
417890UK00004B/138

9 781737 976424